Ashlyn

Marsha Mellow Goes Missing

Marsha Mellow Goes Missing

An Unofficial Story
for Shopkins Collectors

Kenley Shay

Sky Pony Press
New York

First Edition

Visit our website at www.skyponypress.com.

10 9 8 7 6 5 4 3 2 1

Library of Congress Cataloging-in-Publication Data is available on file.

Special thanks to Erin L. Falligant

Cover illustration and design by Jan Gerardi

Print ISBN: 978-1-5107-0251-6
Ebook ISBN: 978-1-5107-0252-3

Printed in Canada

Chapter One

The *jingle* of the front door at Teasley Toys sent Maggie running out from the back room. Were Ava and Bella finally here? No such luck. An older woman in a navy blue trench coat followed a curly-haired toddler into the toy shop.

The little girl ran past the rainbow bookshelf, past the baby dolls and plush pets, and straight to the fire-red train tracks circling the table in the center of the store.

"Is it them?" called Gabby, poking her head out from the back room.

"No," said Maggie—too loudly.

"Shh!" whispered Gran Teasley from behind the counter, raising her finger to her lips. "We have customers, girls."

Maggie sighed and followed her best friend, Gabby, back into the storage room. That's where the Shopkins Kids Club met every Friday afternoon. Gabby's little sister, Ellie, was already sitting on the braided rainbow rug, crinkling a small yellow pouch between her fingers.

"Ellie!" scolded Gabby. "No peeking!"

"I'm not!" said Ellie, whipping the yellow pouch behind her back. She brushed her black bangs out of her eyes with the other hand and stuck out her lower lip.

Maggie couldn't blame her. It was time for the big reveal, and Ava and Bella weren't here! What was keeping them?

She studied her own new purchase: a tiny magenta Shopkins basket with purple handles. It held two yellow pouches—"blind bags," the girls called them. Did they hold an ultra rare Shopkins with crystal glitz? A fluffy baby Shopkins? Or even a limited-edition Shopkins with bling?

Maggie felt a flutter of excitement in her stomach. It was all she could do not to poke at those yellow pouches, but Gabby would bust her for sure. So instead, she pulled the hair band from around her wrist and gathered her ginger-red hair into a low ponytail.

Another *jingle* from the front door brought all three girls to their feet. There was Ava, charging into the shop with her twin sister, Bella, close behind.

"Sorry we're late," fast-talking Ava called to Maggie and the others. "Bella couldn't find her money."

Bella gave a guilty shrug. The two girls looked almost exactly alike, with their curly brown hair, caramel-colored skin, and wide-set eyes. But Ava was the talker and the leader, whereas Bella tended to hang back. Ava said it was because she was born first—a whole three minutes before her "little" sister.

Instead of heading straight to the back room, the two girls ran toward a display of Shopkins that Gran had arranged near the checkout line.

"We just got a new shipment," said Gran. "There could be something special there." She winked at the twins and adjusted her lavender glasses on her nose.

Bella started sifting carefully through the pink packages, but Ava had already chosen. "This one," she said, holding up a five-pack in a clear plastic shell. "It has Fi Fi Flour and Wedgy Wendy. We don't have those two."

Bella nodded and followed Ava to the checkout counter, where the girls pooled their money beside the striped lollipops.

Finally, all five girls were sitting cross-legged in the back room, ready to start this week's official Shopkins Kids Club meeting.

Maggie checked her lime green notebook. "Okay," she said, "Ellie gets to start first today."

Ellie didn't have to be told twice. She tore the edge of her first yellow pouch with her teeth and fished out the contents. "Squeaky Clean!" she shouted, holding up a bitty blue spray bottle.

Maggie slid her finger down her Collector's Guide checklist. "Squeaky Clean is . . . common," she said.

Ellie scrunched up her nose. "Rats," she said. "But he's sure cute." Then she tore open the other yellow pouch. "Ooh . . . shiny!" It was Sour Lemon with crystal glitz.

"Ultra rare!" said Gabby, congratulating her sister. "Good job, Ellie!"

Ellie held Sour Lemon up to the light to watch him sparkle, and then gave him a quick kiss before tucking him safely into the plastic bag by her side.

Gabby opened next. Her first pouch held Dishy Liquid. "Already have that," she said, setting it on the rug. "That's a trader, for sure."

But she squealed when she opened the second pouch and found a fuzzy pink baby bottle. "Aw, Dribbles!" she said, rubbing the soft bottle against her cheek.

Ava and Bella took a turn together, as usual. Ava pulled the tiny yellow pouch out of the bottom of the Shopkins pack and handed it to Bella. "Your turn this week," she said. "*Please* let it be Marsha Mellow. Please, please, please." She closed her eyes and crossed her fingers on both hands.

But it wasn't Marsha Mellow. After Bella snipped the corner of the pouch with scissors, Slick Breadstick dropped out. Bella looked almost apologetic as she held up the little breadstick to show Ava.

"Aw, man. We have him already," said Ava. She sighed and then said, "Oh, well. Twinsies, right, Bella?" Since Ava and Bella shared their Shopkins collection, it was okay to have "twinsies," or two of some things.

I could never share my Shopkins with my little brother, thought Maggie as she ripped open her own pouch. Max was only five and couldn't take care of anything. It would take him about three seconds to lose a Shopkin.

Ava gasped. "Marsha Mellow!" she said, pointing to the Shopkin that had fallen out of Maggie's pouch.

Sure enough, there she was: the prized Marsha Mellow. The limited-edition toasty brown marshmallow was covered in shiny bling.

"We'll trade you for it," Ava said quickly, grabbing the Shopkins lunchbox at her feet. She popped it open and started sorting through her collection. "I'll give you, um, Ma Kettle and . . . Slick Breadstick."

"Hey!" said Bella as Ava grabbed the bread-stick out of her hand. So much for twinsies.

"No, that's not a fair trade," piped up Gabby. "You can only trade a limited-edition for a limited-edition."

Maggie shot her best friend a grateful smile. Everyone knew the rules, but sometimes Ava "forgot"—especially when she was hot after a certain Shopkin.

"I *can't* trade a limited-edition," she whined. "Then I won't have them all!"

Maggie shrugged. "Sorry," she said. "Rules are rules."

An awkward silence followed. Then . . .

Wonk, wonk, wonk!

A remote-controlled fire engine tore into the room, racing across Ellie's plastic bag and toppling Maggie's shopping basket.

Ellie jumped up in surprise, but Maggie didn't budge. She knew exactly who was behind the "fire." "Max!" she bellowed. "Knock it off!"

A freckled face peered around the door-frame. "Oops," he said, grinning and trying to steer the fire truck back out of the room. His fingers fiddled with the controls, but the truck ended up stuck under Gran's desk in the corner.

"Just pick it up!" said Maggie. "We're trying to have a meeting here."

Ellie, who was standing near the desk, crossed her arms and huffed. She was only a year older than Max, but somehow, Maggie could never picture Ellie behaving like him. *Must be a little brother thing*, thought Maggie, wishing for a moment she could trade her sibling as easily as she could trade a Shopkin.

"Fine," said Max, flattening himself onto his stomach to reach beneath the desk. He backed out with the truck in hand and set it down to steer it out of the room remotely.

"Max!" Maggie groaned again. "Just pick it up and carry it!"

Her little brother didn't listen, but he finally managed to steer the truck in a crooked path out the door.

Maggie overheard Mom in the toy shop beyond. Hopefully, she had come early to visit with Gran, not to pick up Maggie. The meeting was just getting started!

"Is Max going camping tomorrow?" asked Ellie, wrinkling her nose at the idea.

"Yes," said Maggie with a sigh. Gran and Papa would never leave Max out of the annual camping trip. But now that the whole Shopkins Kids Club was going, Maggie wished it were girls only—except for Papa, of course.

"Oh, I have a great idea!" said Gabby, rising up on her knees. "You should bring Marsha Mellow camping, especially if we're going to make s'mores around the campfire."

"Yes!" said Ellie. "Marshmallows and Marsha Mellow!"

But before Maggie could respond, Mom appeared in the doorway. Some moms have eagle eyes. Maggie's mom had eagle *ears.*

"I'm not sure that's a good idea, Maggie," she said. "What if you lose your Shopkin at the campsite?"

"But, Mom . . ." Maggie started to protest, until her mother raised an eyebrow in warning.

"Just think about it, okay?" she said. "I know how important your collection is to you. You have to take care of it."

After Mom left, a gloomy cloud seemed to hang over the meeting. What fun would the Shopkins Kids Club campout be without Shopkins?

Maggie fiddled with the purple handle of her plastic basket. Mom said to "think about it." If Maggie wanted to come up with a way to bring her Shopkins, she had to think *fast*—before they all left for the campsite tomorrow.

Chapter Two

"How much farther?" Max whined, wiggling his backpack higher onto his scrawny shoulders.

"Not far," said Papa. "You'll make it." He squatted to secure the yellow tent strapped to his own back. Then he pulled a handkerchief out of his pocket and dabbed the sweat off his flushed forehead.

Maggie and her friends plodded along behind Papa and Max. Gran, carrying a straw picnic basket and wheeling a cooler behind her, brought up the rear. The trail from the parking lot wasn't long, but it was steep and slow going. The late-afternoon sun beat down from the sky above.

When Maggie saw Papa's red face, she grinned and nudged Gabby. "Papa Tomato," she whispered.

Gabby glanced at Papa and giggled.

That's how he had gotten the nickname "Papa" in the first place. He was bald now, but his moustache was ginger-red, the same color as Maggie's hair. His face turned red easily—whenever he was laughing or working hard. With his crimson face, moustache, and glasses, he looked just like Papa Tomato, one of the Shopkins characters.

Gabby had pointed out that Grandma could be "Gran Jam," another Shopkin. And pretty soon, the whole Shopkins Kids Club was calling Maggie's grandparents "Papa" and "Gran." They didn't seem to mind.

Maggie was stepping carefully over a tree root when she heard a yelp from behind her. *Was that Bella?* She and Gabby whirled around.

Bella was lying on her side with Ava sprawled on top of her. Their canvas bag had spilled its contents onto the grass beside the trail.

"Sorry!" said Ava, pulling herself up and brushing dirt off her white capris. "I guess I wore the wrong shoes." Her strappy sandals had little kitten heels—cute, but not great for camping.

As Maggie helped the twins gather their things, she saw Gabby cover a smile. She and

Gabby had both worn sneakers. As they started walking again, Gabby leaned in and said, "This could be a *long* walk."

Luckily, it wasn't.

Just over the hill, Papa stopped, leaned against a tree, and said, "Take a look, girls."

The clearing below spread out before them, lush green and inviting.

Ellie pushed her way to the front of the line and said, "Whoa, pretty."

"But what is that brown spot?" asked Max.

"A fire pit," said Papa. "For our campfire tonight."

"I've got the graham crackers and marshmallows!" Gran sang from behind the group.

Gabby turned suddenly toward Maggie and whispered, "Did you bring her?"

Maggie nodded. Marsha Mellow was zipped safely into the side pocket of her duffel bag.

The Shopkins Kids Club had thought long and hard last night about whether to bring their Shopkins. *You might lose them,* Mom's warning echoed in Maggie's head. So each girl had decided to bring just one—a special Shopkin—for the campout. Maggie couldn't wait to get into the tent to see what the others had brought!

But first, the tent had to be pitched.

Gran set down her basket and helped Papa unroll the butterscotch-colored tent. Then Papa threaded a long pole through the slots. Soon, the yellow dome was reaching toward the sky, with Gran holding it steady while Papa staked it to the ground. They'd been camping for years in this very same spot.

"Can I go in?" asked Max, jumping up and down.

"Just for a minute," said Papa. "Then you're going to help me gather kindling for the fire, right?"

A stack of logs rested beside the fire pit, but Papa liked to gather smaller sticks to get the fire going.

"Right," came Max's muffled voice. His head was already stuck through the zippered doorway.

It was a two-room tent, with space for all five girls on one side of the wall and Max, Gran, and Papa on the other. Maggie couldn't blame Max for wanting to get inside. It was like playing in a giant pineapple.

"C'mon, girls," said Gran. "We have to make one more trip to the car for our sleeping bags."

Maggie sighed. This was the hard part of camping—the carrying in and out.

"Oh," Ava said. "I thought we were done." She was already resting comfortably in the grass, nursing a blister on her heel.

"You stay here, Ava," said Gran kindly. "You can supervise the boys." She winked and then led Maggie and the others back up the trail toward the parking lot.

When they finally had all the sleeping bags and duffel bags tucked into the tent, Papa, Gran, and Max set off into the bushes nearby to find kindling for the fire.

"Anyone else want to help?" asked Papa, poking his head into the tent.

Maggie shook her head. "We have Shopkins Kids Club business to take care of," she said formally. The other girls nodded.

"Sounds serious," said Papa. "I'll leave you to it, then. Holler if you need us." He closed the door flap with a *zzzzzzzzip*.

"Okay!" said Maggie. "What did you bring?"

All the girls rummaged excitedly through their bags and backpacks to pull out their Shopkins.

"Zappy Microwave," Ellie announced, holding up a tiny yellow microwave covered in crystal glitz. "In case we want to make popcorn."

"We would make that over the fire, silly," said Gabby, giggling. "I brought Lana Lamp. It could get dark in here." She held up a bitty raspberry-colored lamp with a glittery gold shade.

"Good idea!" said Ava. She held up a pink high-heeled shoe. "We brought Prommy and . . . Where's yours, Bella?"

Bella dug deep into her shorts pocket and pulled out a matching pink slipper with bunny ears.

"Prommy for daytime and Bun Bun Slipper for night," said Ava. "Now we'll always have something to wear!"

Maggie laughed. Ava sure loved shoes, even if she sometimes wore the wrong kind.

"I brought my Collector's Guidebook, too," said Ava, setting a glossy paperback book on the floor of the tent.

"Cool," said Maggie. Then she held out her own Shopkin. "I, of course, brought Marsha Mellow." She uncurled her fingers to reveal the toasty brown marshmallow in her palm.

Maggie couldn't help but notice the look on Ava's flushed face. She wasn't exactly *green* with envy—more like ruby red—but she looked jealous just the same.

"Wait, I have one more!" said Ellie, holding her hands behind her back.

"Ellie!" scolded Gabby. "You were supposed to bring only one!"

"I know," said Ellie. "But we really, *really* need this one." She slid her hand out in front of her, palm up, and sprung open her fingers. "Leafy!"

She was holding a tiny roll of toilet paper.

All five girls burst out laughing.

"We sure do need that," said Maggie, when she could finally catch her breath. "Or we'll be using *real* leaves!"

That set off another round of giggles.

Soon the girls were in full Shopkins mode. They lined their characters up on top of Ava's book and were talking in teeny-tiny Shopkins voices.

"Hey, girls," said Ava in a high-pitched Prommy voice. "Are there bears around here?" She turned the tiny shoe this way and that, pretending to search the tent for wild animals.

"Yes!" said Maggie in her Marsha Mellow voice, which was low and toasty. "And they like to eat marshmallows." She shook Marsha as if she were trembling with fear.

"And, um, bears eat bunnies, too," Bella whispered. She hopped Bun Bun over to meet Marsha and Prommy.

"Yes, they do!" said Ava, encouraging her twin. Prommy and Bun Bun huddled side by side.

"It's getting kind of dark," said Ellie—in her normal voice. Except she sounded worried. Was all this bear talk scaring her?

Maggie glanced up at the clear window in the top of the tent. The sun had sunk behind the tree line, casting a dark shadow across the tent floor. She shivered. "Lana Lamp, can you shine some light on things?" she asked Gabby.

"Sure!" said Gabby in her bright, cheery Lana Lamp voice. She pretended to pull the string on the little lamp. "There, see?" she said to Ellie. "No bears here."

Ellie chewed her thumbnail. She glanced around the shadowy tent. "When will Gran and Papa be back?" she asked in a small voice.

"Soon," said Maggie, trying to reassure her.

But Ellie's fear must have been contagious.

"Do you think there really *are* bears out here?" asked Ava, pulling Prommy back onto her lap.

Maggie was about to say no, when something scratched against the side of the tent.

The girls froze.

There it was again: a soft scratching noise coming from behind Maggie. She jumped and whirled around. With the next scratch, the tent wall quivered, as if a paw were prodding it. A paw with giant claws . . .

Chapter Three

All five girls tumbled into the opposite corner of the tent. Someone's sharp elbow pressed into Maggie's back, but she didn't care. She couldn't get far enough away from that . . . that *thing* that was trying to get into the tent.

Ellie started whimpering.

"What do we do?" whispered Gabby.

Ava had her eyes shut tight, as if that would make the animal go away. Bella's eyes were wide open, though, when she whispered, "Be quiet. Be very, very quiet."

They all froze, sitting in silence. Maggie couldn't quiet her breath. It was coming in short, fast huffs.

The animal pawed the tent again and pressed its nose against the nylon, trying to find a way in. Maggie shrank back.

Then she noticed something about the face that was outlined in smooth yellow fabric. "It's not an animal," she whispered. "It's a man!"

Another second passed, and she said, "It's not a man. It's a *boy.* Max!" Maggie sprang to her feet in anger.

The face pressed further into the wall of the tent and slowly stuck out its tongue. "Gross!" said Ellie, but she sounded relieved.

Maggie raced for the opening of the tent, but by the time she got outside, Max was gone, sprinting toward Papa and the fire pit. "Good!" she called to him. "And stay away!"

But he didn't.

When the girls had finally calmed down and gotten back to their Shopkins, Max stepped just outside the zippered door and said, "Knock, knock. Can I play, too?"

"No," Maggie snapped.

Max unzipped the door anyway and stuck his freckled face inside. "Can I watch?"

"No!" she said, leaping up to zip the door shut.

Maggie could still see Max's outline sitting next to the tent. "Can I listen?" he asked in his sweetest voice.

"No!" all five girls yelled together.

The shape on the other side of the tent got up and stomped away, sulking. *Finally.*

"Girls, come eat!" Gran called.

The smell of roasting hot dogs wafted into the tent, luring the girls outside.

"Should we bring our Shopkins?" asked Ellie, holding up Zappy Microwave.

"No," said Gabby. "We're leaving them in the tent to keep them safe, remember?"

Ellie's shoulders sank. "Okay," she said. "But I really wanted popcorn."

Gabby shook her head. "You know that microwave doesn't really work, right? And if it did, it could only pop like *one* kernel at a time."

Ellie giggled.

"Besides," said Maggie, "we have something *better* than popcorn for tonight. S'mores!"

Ellie cheered as she set down Zappy Microwave. "Check you later!" she called to her toy, using the closing line from the Shopkins cartoon.

"Check you later!" the other girls echoed as they filed out of the tent toward the glow of the campfire.

When they got there, Gran handed out long sticks with sharpened ends. Max already had his stick, with a hot dog perched on the end, resting in the flames.

"Not too close to the fire," said Papa, sitting beside him. "It'll burn."

Max pulled his hot dog back and glanced smugly at Maggie as if he were holding some great treasure.

Gran slid a cold hot dog onto the end of Ava's stick, and Ava's nose wrinkled. "We have to cook them?" she asked. She held the stick away from her as though it were a petrified snake.

"You don't *have* to," said Gran. "But it's kind of fun, isn't it?"

The look on Ava's face said it was anything *but* fun.

"No worries," said Gran. "Papa has already cooked a few. Grab a bun from the bag and he'll put a hot dog in it."

Ava handed her stick to Bella, who happily took it. "I think I'm going to wash my hands first," said Ava, brushing her hands together.

"That's a fine idea," said Gran. "The water bucket's over by the tent."

The rest of the girls took spots on the log benches around the fire. The flames sparked and crackled, roasting the hot dogs to a deep reddish-brown. Maggie's stomach growled. They smelled delicious!

When her hot dog was roasted to perfection, Papa helped her slide it into a bun. She lined it with catsup—no mustard, thank you very much—and then took her first, satisfying bite.

"Ooh, that looks good," said Gabby. "I wish mine would hurry up." She rotated her stick and then gazed upward. "Wow, look how bright the stars are out here!"

"I know," said Maggie, glancing up and trying not to talk too much with her mouth full. Everything seemed clearer in the woods: the stars sparkling in the sky; the twitter of birds and insects in the trees; the smell of burning firewood; and especially, the taste of these roasted hot dogs. She took another bite.

The hot dogs were so good that even Ava had two. "Save room for s'mores," Gran warned.

"No problem there," said Maggie, wiping catsup off her fingers with a napkin. "There's always room for s'more!"

Gabby laughed. Maggie could always count on her best friend for that.

"Max, want to help me get the s'more fixings?" asked Gran, pushing herself up from the log. He trailed her back toward the tent.

Soon those sharpened hot dog sticks had become marshmallow sticks, held low over the flames with marshmallows stuck to the ends.

"Ellie, don't burn yours!" Gabby warned. "Hold it over here like mine."

Ellie shook her head. "I like it burned," she said.

All the girls watched as Ellie's marshmallow caught fire and bulged into a black, crispy bubble. When it had cooled, Papa helped her slide the melted lump between two graham crackers alongside a square of chocolate.

Did Ellie really like it burned or just like it *fast*? Maggie wasn't sure. But Ellie gobbled it up in no time and then reached for another marshmallow from the plastic bag.

As Gabby put together a s'more, Maggie tried to be patient. Her own marshmallow was just beginning to brown up. "How's this?" she asked the other girls.

"Perfect," said Ava, turning her stick slowly in the fire pit below.

"Perfectly toasty," added Gabby. She took a gooey bite of her s'more and then said, "It wux wike motsa-meh-wo."

"Huh?" asked Maggie, giggling.

Gabby laughed, too, and clapped her hand over her mouth. She chewed quickly, swallowed hard, and then said again, "It looks like Marsha Mellow."

"Oh!" said Maggie. "I guess it does."

Ava leaned over. "Not quite," she said. "Marsha Mellow is way more *yellow*. Oh, hey! That rhymed!"

Maggie studied her marshmallow. "Really? Yellow?" she said.

"Definitely," said Ava. "Don't you think so, Bella?"

Bella was eating her s'more sideways, licking the marshmallow that dripped over the edge. She shrugged.

"Marsha is golden *brown*," said Gabby firmly. "Why don't you go get her so we can see, Maggie?"

Maggie hesitated. She'd promised herself—and her mom—that she'd leave her Shopkin in the tent.

"You don't have to check," Ava snapped. "She's yellow. I've been studying her in my Collector's Guidebook for weeks now."

Gabby clamped her mouth shut.

Maggie glanced from Ava to her best friend and back again. Someone had to settle this once and for all.

"I'll be right back," said Maggie. "Here, watch my marshmallow." She handed her roasting stick to Gabby and hurried toward the tent.

"Wait," said Gran. "If you're heading that way, take a flashlight." She pulled out a long silver flashlight from the bag at her feet and handed it to Maggie.

Maggie switched the flashlight on and followed the bouncing beam across the grass toward the tent. It was hard to wiggle the zipper down while holding the flashlight in her hand, but she managed. Then she crawled inside and made her way toward her sleeping bag in the corner.

The girls had left their Shopkins lined up in a row on Ava's Collector's Guidebook.

Prommy and Bun Bun Slipper were sitting in front of Zappy Microwave, waiting for their popcorn. Lana Lamp was in the middle of the book, lighting the "room." And Leafy was off in the corner, where Ellie had decided the bathroom should be.

But where was Marsha Mellow? Had she fallen off?

Maggie used the flashlight to search around the book. She lifted the edge of her sleeping bag. She searched under her duffel.

Then she searched under Gabby's sleeping bag. And around her backpack. And under her backpack.

By the time Maggie had searched under the last sleeping bag in the tent, her heart was pounding in her ears.

Marsha Mellow wasn't there.

Marsha Mellow was *missing*.

Chapter Four

"It's just a toy," Gran said soothingly, rubbing Maggie's back.

Maggie pulled away, horrified. "No, it's *not,*" she said. "It's Marsha Mellow!"

"A limited-edition Marsha Mellow!" said Ava, who seemed even more offended than Maggie.

"With bling!" piped up Ellie.

Gran raised her eyebrows. "Oh, I see," she said. "You're right. This is an important matter." She glanced at Papa as if looking for help, but he was busy tending the fire.

"Well," said Gran, "we should definitely look for Miss Marsha Mellow. But I think we would have better luck in the morning, when it's light out."

"No!" wailed Maggie. "Please, Gran. Can't we look now? She could be gone by morning!"

"Yeah," said Gabby quietly. "She's shiny. I heard that birds like shiny things. They might steal Marsha Mellow and take her to their nest."

Maggie snapped her head sideways to look at Gabby. "For real?" she said.

Gabby nodded solemnly.

"Or even *bats,*" added Ava. "They might take her back to their cave—or wherever." She ducked her head a little as she glanced toward the sky.

Maggie's jaw dropped open. This was going from bad to worse fast. "We have to find her, Gran!" she wailed.

Gran sighed. "Okay, where did you see her last?"

"In the tent," said Maggie quickly. "But I already looked."

"We'll look again," Gran said, getting up from the log. She pressed her hand against her lower back as she walked toward the tent. She clearly wasn't happy about this search, but Maggie was glad for her help. "C'mon, girls," Gran called over her shoulder.

While Gran held the flashlight overhead, all five girls searched their things. They shook out their sleeping bags, hoping something would fall. They poked around in the pockets of their backpacks and duffel bags. They ran their hands along the floor of the tent, wondering if Marsha Mellow was hiding in a corner—the way the girls had during the "bear attack" earlier that day.

But eventually, even Gran had to admit it: Marsha Mellow wasn't here.

Maggie sank down to her knees. *Now what?*

"We could look outside," said Gabby. "Maybe you accidentally brought her with you when we went to the campfire for dinner?"

It sounded pretty far-fetched, but Maggie was willing to try anything at this point. So the girls used all three of Gran's flashlights to search the area near the campfire.

Papa and Max, who were poking the dying embers with their sticks, searched near their benches, too.

There were lots of shiny things in the grass. Bella found a soda-can tab. Gabby found a nickel. And Ava found a hunk of shiny wet hot dog.

"Ew, disgusting!" she said, flinging it from her fingers.

After they'd combed every inch of the grass, Gran said the words Maggie dreaded hearing.

"We can look again in the morning. It's too dark to find anything tonight."

Maggie fought back hot tears. Then she felt a heavy hand on her shoulder. It was Papa.

"I'm sorry, Magpie," he said, using his pet name for her. "Would it help if we put one more log on the fire and sang some campfire songs?"

Maggie sniffled and shrugged.

As Papa fed the fire with small twigs and branches, Maggie's friends tried to cheer her up, too.

"Should we make up songs about our Shopkins?" asked Ellie with a sweet smile.

Maggie's chest tightened.

"Shh, Ellie!" said Gabby, whirling around to silence her sister. "That won't make Maggie feel better. Her Shopkin is lost, remember?"

"Oh," said Ellie. "Sorry." She sank down onto a log like a turtle retreating into its shell. Maggie almost felt sorry for her.

"Should I bring out my Collector's Guidebook?" asked Ava, gesturing toward the tent. "Instead of talking about the Shopkins we have, we could dream about all the Shopkins we still want!"

Maggie shook her head. The only Shopkin she was dreaming about right now was Marsha

Mellow. She sighed and rested her chin in her hands.

"Yeah, I guess that won't help either," said Ava, squatting down onto a log beside her sister.

Gabby still held the silver flashlight in her hand. She flicked it on and off, her brow furrowed in deep thought. Suddenly, she turned the flashlight on full beam and held it under her chin like a microphone. "We interrupt this campout to bring you a special report," she said in her deepest voice.

All the others turned to look at Gabby, her face orange with light. Ellie giggled. Even Maggie was curious. What was her best friend doing?

Gabby cleared her throat and continued. "The Shopkins Kids Club is in total chaos after a tragic disappearance. The one and only Marsha Mellow was reported missing just an hour or so ago. We turn now to Ava for a live report."

She swung the flashlight over to Ava, who took the "microphone" in surprise. She stared at Gabby blankly until Bella leaned over and whispered something in Ava's ear. Ava's eyes lit up.

"Oh!" she said. "I get it—this is like that Shopkins cartoon where the shopping cart got tipped over and Apple Blossom did the special report to find the villain who did it and—"

"Yes!" said Gabby impatiently. "But our audience is waiting. Ava, can you tell us anything more about the mysterious disappearance of Marsha Mellow?"

Ava held the flashlight under her chin and said, "I certainly can, Gabriella. We all admired Marsha Mellow. She was a limited-edition—the real deal. She was a toasty yellow color and was the blingiest of the blingy Shopkins. Wait, is *blingiest* a word?"

Ava turned toward Bella, who shrugged. But that gave Gabby enough time to take back the microphone.

"Thank you for that, um, very *special* report," she said. "But we're running out of time, folks."

Maggie was glad. If she had to hear one more word about how *blingy* Marsha Mellow was, she was afraid she might throw up.

"What our audience really wants to know," said Gabby, "is what happened? Where is Marsha Mellow? Margaret was the last person to see the missing Shopkin. Margaret, can you tell us where you were and what you were doing?"

She held out the flashlight to Maggie, who paused for a moment before taking it. She cleared her throat. "Um, yes, Gabriella, I can. But please call me 'Maggie.'"

Gabby nodded and whispered, "Sorry."

Maggie thought back to that afternoon, which now seemed like it had been days ago. "Marsha Mellow was last seen here in the Crystal Lake Woods," she began in a hushed tone, feeling the warmth of the bright light on her face. "She was camping out with her closest friends, Prommy and Bun Bun Slipper."

Gabby nodded, a serious expression on her face. She reached for the flashlight and asked, "Margaret—er, Maggie—are detectives closing in on a suspect?"

"A suspect?" asked Maggie.

"Um, yeah," said Gabby. "You know, like a kidnapper."

Maggie's mind started spinning. Did Gabby think someone stole Marsha Mellow?

Ava stood up. "There were reports of a wild bear loose in the campsite," she said, raising her arms dramatically.

"A bear?" Max whimpered from the woodpile, where he was helping Gran and Papa straighten up the logs.

"No, Maxxy," said Gran. "No bears here."

Gabby spoke more quietly into the "microphone." "You heard it here, folks," she said. "No bears. But some witnesses thought that a large bird or a bat might have taken Marsha Mellow."

All the girls glanced quickly overhead.

"A bat?" squeaked Max. Boy, that kid had good ears!

Gran spoke up again. "Try not to scare Max, girls," she gently scolded.

Ava sighed as if to say, *Well, there goes all our fun.*

But Gabby didn't miss a beat. "Maggie," she asked in a serious tone, "are there any people you know who might have wanted to steal Marsha Mellow?"

Everyone fell silent. Maggie listened to the crackle of the flames in front of her as she chewed on the question. She'd been so busy trying to figure out where she'd lost Marsha Mellow. It hadn't even occurred to her that someone might have taken her special Shopkin.

Who would do that?

Maggie didn't have to ask herself twice. There was only one person who'd wanted Marsha Mellow even more than Maggie had. And that person was sitting right across the fire from her.

Ava.

Chapter Five

"Maggie?" Gabby waved the flashlight under Maggie's chin to get her attention. "Do you know anyone who would want to steal Marsha Mellow?"

Maggie's mouth went dry. All eyes were on her as she tried to swallow—and to avoid looking across the fire at Ava.

Ellie broke the silence, as usual.

"Ava really wants Marsha Mellow!" she said, bouncing a little on her log.

Now Ellie was the one in the hot seat. As the other girls whirled around to look at Ellie, Maggie snuck a peek at Ava, whose mouth had dropped open.

"Me?" she said. "Hey! I didn't steal Marsha Mellow!"

"Well, you really want her, though," said Ellie defensively.

No one could argue with that.

Gabby flickered the flashlight to break the awkward silence. "That's, um, really all we have time for, folks. We'll continue to investigate the case of the missing Marsha Mellow. But now, it's time for . . . the weather."

When Gabby thrust the flashlight into Maggie's hands, Maggie almost dropped it like a hot potato. This conversation had gone from fun to not-so-friendly way too fast. So as she raised the flashlight to her face, all she could say was "The weather report? It's . . . um . . . getting hot out here."

Then she flicked off the flashlight. The news was over, but the questions bouncing around in her head had just begun.

John Jacob Jingleheimer Schmidt,
His name is my *name, too.*
Whenever we go out,
The people always shout,
"There goes John Jacob Jingleheimer Schmidt!"
Na na na na na na na . . .

Max sang the loudest, and he did a little dance at the "na na na" part. But as he and the others started up the next round, Maggie fell silent. The new log in the fire pit was blazing now, casting flickering shadows across the faces of her friends. She looked from one to the next, her gaze settling on Ava.

Ava was not only singing, but she was dancing on her log, shimmying her shoulders and leaning into Bella. She was having so much fun—way different from how Maggie felt right now.

Ava looks like she just opened a Shopkins basket and found Marsha Mellow, Maggie couldn't help thinking.

She tried to shake off the thought, but it kept niggling at the back of her mind. Had Ava stolen Marsha Mellow from her?

As Maggie stared at Ava, hot, angry flames began to rise in her chest. The longer she sat, the more sure she was that she'd found the culprit. She finally sat up straight and grabbed Gabby's hand, making Gabby jump.

"C'mon," said Maggie in a fierce whisper.

"Where are we going?" asked Gabby, trying to tug back her hand.

"Just follow me." Maggie sprang up from the log and marched through the darkness toward the tent.

After they'd unzipped the flap and were safely crouched inside, Maggie spilled her suspicions to Gabby. "I think Ava *did* steal Marsha Mellow!" she whispered.

"No way," said Gabby, shaking her head.

"Yes way," Maggie insisted. "It had to be her! Remember how much she was dying to get Marsha Mellow?"

"Yeah, but . . ." began Gabby.

"Think about it," said Maggie, kneeling and putting her hands on Gabby's shoulders to look her square in the eyes. "Ava was the only one who went back to the tent before dinner. Remember how she wanted to wash her hands?"

Gabby's brown eyes widened. "Yeah," she said, "I remember." Then she just shook her head again. "But that doesn't mean Ava snuck into the tent and stole Marsha Mellow. She probably really was washing her hands. You know she doesn't like to touch anything gross."

Maggie fell back on her bottom in disgust. Whose side was Gabby on, anyway?

Someone started fiddling with the tent's zipper, and both girls froze.

"Hey, let me in!" squeaked Ellie, like a little pig trying to get into a straw house instead of keeping the big bad wolf out of it.

"Just a minute!" Gabby said, shushing her sister.

"But it's dark out here!" Ellie whimpered.

Gabby sighed. "We should probably go back out," she said.

Maggie felt like a balloon that had been popped. Her best friend didn't believe that Ava had stolen Marsha Mellow. *That just means I'll have to find a way to prove it*, she thought.

Later that night, as all the girls were safely tucked into their sleeping bags, Maggie stared at the ceiling of the tent and tried to make a plan. She would have to sneak back into the tent tomorrow, alone. She would go through Ava's canvas bag in search of her toasty little friend.

I'll rescue Marsha Mellow if it's the last thing I do, vowed Maggie, closing her eyes. Then she let the rhythm of Papa's snoring soothe her to sleep.

She dreamed of Marsha Mellow, teetering on the edge of a long stick over a pit of flames.

The stick was bouncing, and Marsha Mellow was wobbling back and forth like a tightrope walker.

"Hang on!" called Maggie, lunging for the stick.

Wonk, wonk, wonk!

A tiny fire engine raced toward the fire pit, with an even tinier Max at the wheel.

The sound startled Marsha Mellow, and with one backward somersault, she tumbled off the stick and into the hot fire.

"No!" cried Maggie. She untangled the hose from the fire truck and tried to spray the flames, but all that came out of the itty-bitty hose was a trickle of water. *Drip, drip, drip . . .*

"No!" cried Maggie again, sitting straight up in her sleeping bag. She opened her eyes.

The tent was cool, dark, and silent—except for the *drip, drip, drip* of raindrops on the nylon roof overhead.

Gabby stirred in the sleeping bag next to Maggie, but the other girls were sleeping soundly. So Maggie lay back down, taking deep, steady breaths to calm her racing heart.

I have to find Marsha Mellow, she thought sadly. *I have to!*

Chapter Six

"*Muckity, muck, muck, muck*," said Max, sliding his tennis shoes through the wet, muddy grass around the fire pit. The bottoms of his cargo pants were splattered with dirty drops.

"Get out of there, Maxwell," scolded Papa. "Don't get yourself all muddy."

But it was hard not to. Maggie glanced down at her own purple sneakers, which were already dark with dew. The rain had stopped early that morning, but everything at the campsite felt damp and cold.

Gran put down plastic bags on the logs around the fire pit so the girls could sit and eat their breakfast.

As Maggie slowly peeled her banana, she scanned the dark, wet ashes of the fire pit. She remembered her dream from the night before and shivered in the damp air. *Was Marsha Mellow in that pit somewhere, burned to a crisp? Or had she been hidden away in the shadows by the hands of a sneaky thief?*

Maggie glanced sideways at Ava, who was biting into a powdered sugar doughnut. White sugar dust sprinkled down onto her jean shorts.

Maggie sighed. Too bad Ava hadn't left a trail of doughnut crumbs leading to Marsha Mellow.

"What are you thinking?" asked Gabby, nudging Maggie's shoulder. "You look so serious."

Maggie shrugged and took a bite of banana.

Then Ellie wiped off her juice moustache with the back of her hand and said, "She's thinking about Marsha Mellow." For a six-year-old, she was pretty smart.

Bella nodded and gave Maggie a sympathetic smile. But Ava just flicked a crumb off her lap and took another big bite of doughnut.

"Well," said Gran, cupping a steaming mug of coffee, "our job today is to help Maggie think about something other than Marsha Mellow. We have most of the day to enjoy the woods. How about a hike over to Crystal Lake, girls?"

"Yes!" said Ellie. She jumped up so fast she spilled a dribble of juice down her shirt.

No! thought Maggie. *I don't want to leave the tent. I don't want to leave Marsha Mellow!* But then she had another thought. If Ava were hiking, that would give Maggie the chance she needed—the chance to sneak into the tent and find her Shopkin.

"Let's do it!" she said, faking excitement.

"Really?" said Gran. "I'm pleased to hear that, Maggie. I'm proud of you."

Maggie felt a little guilty. Would Gran be proud if she knew Maggie's real plan? Probably not. But Marsha Mellow was counting on her. Maggie took her last bite of banana and threw the peel into the trash bag.

Before long, the girls were all lined up and ready to take the trail over to Crystal Lake. Birds twittered overhead as they followed Gran and Papa, who carried a fishing pole, toward the dirt path through the woods.

Maggie dragged her feet, bringing up the rear of the hiking party.

"What's going on with you?" asked Gabby, tugging Maggie's sleeve. "Are you tired or something?"

Maggie shook her head and raised her finger to her lips. She hadn't filled Gabby in on her plan. Was Gabby going to blow it for her? Maggie picked up her pace—just a little.

As the hikers neared the first bend in the trail, she saw her chance. "Um, Gran?" she said. "I need to run back to the tent for my sunscreen." It was the best excuse she could come up with.

Gran shook her head and patted the shoulder bag she carried. "I have some right here," she said. She reached inside to find the bottle.

Maggie's stomach sank. She should have known Gran would be ultra-prepared. Now what?

"Um, yeah, but I need my hat, too," she said quickly, her voice cracking. "The sun's hurting my eyes."

Gran looked up at the morning sun filtering down through the tree leaves. She glanced over her shoulder at Papa, who was leading the hike. Max walked beside him, digging at the ground with a long stick.

Finally, Gran turned back and said, "Go on, then, Maggie. But take a friend. We'll wait for you here."

Maggie looked at Gabby, her eyes pleading. "C'mon," she said. "Please?"

Gabby shrugged. "Fine," she said, "but I don't think the sun's all that bright, really . . ."

Maggie reached for her friend's hand, wishing she would stop talking. She pulled Gabby back down the trail, skipping over a mud puddle or two.

"Check you later!" she heard Ava call to their backs.

No, I'll check you *later,* thought Maggie. *Your things, anyway.*

When she and Gabby had jogged far enough from the others, Maggie said, "I don't really need my hat. I'm going back for something else."

By the time they reached the tent, Maggie had explained her plan to Gabby—and Gabby was not happy.

"Margaret Josephine!" she said, putting her hands on her hips and sounding just like Maggie's mom. "Are you really going to search through Ava's things?"

"Yup," said Maggie quickly. She didn't have time to explain it to Gabby—or to try to convince her. Gran and the others were waiting.

Maggie unzipped the tent and headed straight for Bella and Ava's canvas bag. She dumped it upside down on the tent floor, rummaging through the clothes, searching for anything small, plastic, and hard. She found a wide-toothed comb, two toothbrushes, and a tube of lip balm.

By the time Gabby squatted down beside her, Maggie was shaking the canvas bag, hoping something else would drop out. Then she spotted the zipper pocket on the side. The pocket held something hard and lumpy.

Maggie glanced up at Gabby, expecting her to tell her to stop digging and put everything back as they'd found it. But she didn't. Gabby must have seen the lumps in that pocket, too, because her eyes were gleaming with curiosity.

"Hurry up already!" Gabby said impatiently.

Maggie unzipped the pocket and reached her fingers inside. She felt the sharp heel of a shoe and promptly pulled out pink Prommy. The face on the shoe was grinning at her as if to say, "Fooled you!"

Maggie reached in again, feeling two more objects bouncing against each other. The ears on one told her, before she even pulled it out, that she was holding Bun Bun Slipper.

But the last lump was smooth. It was kind of square. And as Maggie pulled it out, she felt a tingle of excitement run down her spine.

"Hey!" someone shouted.

As Ava crawled into the tent on all fours, Maggie flung her hand behind her back.

"I needed a Band-Aid," said Ava, unbuckling her sandal. But as soon as she saw what Maggie and Gabby were doing, her smile turned upside down.

"Hey," she said again, more slowly this time. "Are you . . . going through my stuff?" She glanced from Maggie to Gabby, and back again.

Gabby stared at the floor of the tent.

Maggie tried to speak, but her throat had gone dry. "Um . . ." She cleared her throat. "We . . . were just looking for my hat."

"In my bag?" Ava said, pointing. "No you weren't. You were looking for something else. What for?" Then a dark curtain fell across her face, and she sprang to her feet. "You were looking for Marsha Mellow!" she said accusingly. "You think I stole your Shopkin!"

Maggie felt like a damp sponge that had just been wrung out. All she could do was nod limply.

Ava crossed her arms. "Well?" she said, her eyes flashing. "What did you find?"

Maggie swallowed hard and brought her hand back out in front of her. She uncurled her fingers and glanced down at the . . . square of wrapped strawberry candy.

"Taffy," said Ava evenly. "You found taffy—which I would have shared with you if you'd just asked. If you'd trusted me. If . . ." Her face crumpled suddenly, and she turned and ran out of the tent.

Maggie could barely look at Gabby. When she did, she saw anger flash across Gabby's face, too.

"I told you," said Gabby. "I told you Ava didn't take your Shopkin, and now she thinks you don't trust her. She thinks *we* don't trust her!"

After Gabby stormed out of the tent behind Ava, Maggie sunk onto her knees. She refolded Ava's and Bella's clothes, piece by piece, and tucked them carefully back into the bag. When she heard Gran calling to her from outside the tent, she jumped to her feet and braced herself for yet another scolding.

She looked down and realized she was still holding the taffy in her sweaty palm—the fruit-flavored candy that she'd mistaken for Marsha Mellow.

Maggie wanted to stamp on that candy until it broke into a thousand pieces. She wanted to fling it miles away into the woods. But, really, how could she be mad at a piece of candy? Instead, she tucked it back into the zippered pocket of the canvas bag, next to Prommy and Bun Bun Slipper.

"Check you later," Maggie whispered to them as she zipped up the pocket. "That is, if I'm not totally grounded."

She sighed and crawled out of the tent to face the wrath of Gran.

Chapter Seven

"Did you find your hat?" asked Gran, her voice edged with concern. The blinding morning sun poured over her shoulder, making it difficult to see her face clearly. But she didn't seem mad. Not in the slightest.

Ava must not have told her what happened!

Maggie thought fast. "I . . . guess I didn't bring my hat," she said, standing up outside the tent and brushing off her shorts with her hands. "I'll take some of that sunscreen, though!" she said brightly—a little too brightly.

Gran cocked her head to one side. "All right," she said, reaching for her bag. "But your friends are waiting, Maggie. Time's a ticking."

Maggie took the tiniest squirt of sunscreen from Gran's orange bottle and rubbed it on her nose. Then she took off jogging toward the group of girls waiting beside the trail.

When Maggie reached her friends, Gabby wouldn't look at her. She was digging her sneaker into the dirt of the trail. And Ava was in the lead, already hiking up the trail, with Bella jogging along behind her. Maybe Ava didn't have time to wait for someone who thought she was, well, a thief.

Only Ellie smiled and waved at Maggie—until she took a good look at Maggie's bare head. "Hey!" she said. "Where's your hat?" Maggie shrugged and tried to change the subject. "Should we collect some, um"—she quickly scanned the trail—"some rocks, Ellie? Look at this one!" Maggie bent over to pick up a grayish-purple stone. It was a geode, the kind that Papa sometimes cracked open to reveal the crystals inside.

But by the time she stood back up again, Ellie was gone. She was hiking ahead up the trail, hand in hand, with Gabby.

Maggie stood still, watching them all go—the two sets of sisters, side by side, and Papa and Max, too far ahead to even see anymore. She felt a sharp pang of loneliness. Then she heard Gran's comforting voice from behind.

"You okay, Mags?" Gran asked kindly.

Maggie nodded, afraid that if she spoke, she would cry. She slid the gray rock into her pocket and walked on a few steps ahead of Gran, hoping her grandmother wouldn't see her face. She didn't want to confess that she'd just broken not one friendship, but two—cracked open like dull gray stones on the ground below.

"Sharks!" Max squealed, trying to balance on the rocks along the shore of Crystal Lake. He dipped in one bare toe and quickly pulled it out again.

Ellie climbed onto the moss-covered rocks beside him, under Gran's watchful eye.

"Careful, kids," Gran called from her blanket on the grassy shore. "Those might be slippery!"

Gabby, Ava, and Bella had followed Papa out to the end of a long pier, where he was prepping his fishing pole.

Maggie hung back, watching from shore. With the sun glinting off the water, she could see why it had been named "Crystal Lake." If she could gather up those "diamonds" sparkling on the water, she could buy all the Shopkins she'd ever wanted. *Including a new Marsha Mellow for me*, she thought. *And maybe one for Ava.*

Ava hadn't so much as looked her way since they'd set out on the trail. Maggie fought another wave of sadness rising in her chest. She took a deep, shaky breath and walked out onto the pier.

Gabby sat on one side, her legs dangling down toward the water.

"Are you going to fish?" Maggie asked, squatting beside her. She was thrilled when Gabby actually looked her way.

"Nah," said Gabby. "I heard there are sharks in this lake." Her face was dead serious for a moment, and then she broke into a lop-sided smile.

Maggie giggled. "I heard there were whales!" It felt so good to be laughing with her best friend again.

When Papa offered her the fishing pole, she took it. She stood up and cast the lure as far out as she could, and then watched the red and white bobber float peacefully on the water's surface. Papa had taken Maggie fishing lots of times, only usually Max was elbowing her out of the way to get a turn.

Why wasn't he doing that today?

Maggie glanced to her left at the rocky shoreline. Max and Ellie were playing together happily—for the first time ever. If those two could get along, it gave Maggie hope that maybe she and Ava could make peace, too.

"Do you want to take a turn, Ava?" she asked, looking along the other side of the pier, where Ava and Bella were sitting together. She figured Ava would say no. The last thing that girl would want to touch would be a worm or a slimy fish. But it couldn't hurt to ask.

Ava narrowed her eyes at Maggie. She licked her lips and then said slowly, "No, thank you. I wouldn't want you to think that I *stole* your fish."

Ouch.

So much for making peace. . . .

When the pole bounced in Maggie's hands, she quickly began reeling in the lure.

"Looks like you've got something!" said Papa, holding on to his hat as if they were in a boat, reeling in a big one.

Gabby sprang to her feet to stand beside Maggie, shading her eyes to see what might be on the other end of the line. Even Ava and Bella turned toward the end of the pier, watching silently.

As the "fish" got closer, though, something felt off. Maggie gave a little tug on the line, expecting the fish to tug back. Instead, the line just felt, well, stuck. She tugged a little more and then felt the line break free. She easily reeled it in the rest of the way.

As the lure lifted out of the water, a long strand of green algae dangled below it, drip, drip, dripping green droplets into the lake.

"Oh, my favorite!" Papa said with a chuckle. "Swamp fish. Should we have Gran fry it up for lunch?"

"Gross," muttered Ava. But Bella smiled a little over her sister's shoulder.

Luckily, Gran had something else in mind for lunch. When the sun was high in the sky, she unpacked some snacks on her blanket and made room for everyone to sit around her. Ava was the last one to "the table." Even Bella, who was glancing eagerly at Gran's picnic basket, made it to the blanket first.

When the only spot left was next to Maggie, Ava chose to sit in the grass, instead.

Maggie didn't have time to worry about that. She was suddenly starving. She heaped up her paper plate with cheese and cracker sandwiches and purple grapes.

Ellie crunched on a carrot stick and reached into the plastic bag for another one. "Hey, look at this!" she said, holding up the carrot. It had a bulge on one end and then got really skinny toward the other. "It looks like . . . a microphone!"

She held it up to her mouth and said, "Ladies and gentlemen. We interrupt this picnic to bring you a special report."

Uh-oh, thought Maggie. *Not this again.*

"Marsha Mellow is still missing!" said Ellie, spitting a little piece of carrot onto the picnic blanket.

"Ellie, don't talk with your mouth full," Gabby scolded, trying to grab the carrot.

But Ellie was on a roll. She stood up and held the carrot out toward Max. "We go to my friend, Max, now for more important information."

Max took the carrot proudly. He seemed glad to be included—for once. He held up the carrot and looked skyward, as if trying to think of something *important* to say.

"Max," said Ellie, prompting him. "Do you know what happened to Marsha Mellow?"

Max shrugged. He looked down at the carrot stick and then back at Ellie.

"Max," she said again. "Do you know who stole Marsha Mellow?"

Ava sighed and got up abruptly from the grass. She walked toward the pier, leaving her plate of cheese and crackers behind.

"Ellie, stop that," pleaded Gabby.

Maggie reached for the carrot stick in Max's hand. Then she noticed something. Max's face was red and kind of scrunched up, the way it got when he was just about to cry. *Why was he upset?*

Ellie wouldn't let it go. She was like a real reporter, chasing down clues. "Max," she said quietly, leaning toward him. "This is really, *really* important. Do you know who stole Marsha Mellow?"

That did it. Max's mouth quivered, and then his whole freckled face burst into tears. He threw the carrot stick to the ground and ran toward the trail. Ellie watched him go, her mouth open wide.

"What was that all about?" asked Gran, turning to Maggie.

Maggie raised her palms. "Who knows?" she said. "He's a baby sometimes, but that . . . was just weird." She'd thought he and Ellie were finally hitting it off. He was playing Shopkins with Maggie and her friends, or at least pretending to be in a Shopkins cartoon. So why would he run away?

Normally, she'd let Max cry for a while until he was ready to talk about what was bothering him. But something about the way he was acting today felt different.

"I'll go look for him," Maggie said, rising to her feet. As she walked toward the trail, she expected to see Max waiting just over the hill, pouting like a toddler waiting to be picked up and cuddled.

But he wasn't there.

She glanced down the dirt trail, as far as her eyes could see. No Max.

A ball of worry started to gather in Maggie's stomach. This wasn't normal little brother behavior. Something was definitely wrong.

Chapter Eight

"Max!" Maggie called, jogging along the dirt path back toward the campsite. *Where was he?*

Her little brother was fast, but she was still faster. Why hadn't she caught up to him by now?

Maggie's breath was coming in short bursts. She wanted to stop and walk, but she had to find her little brother. Worry nagged at her, making her speed up even more. She kept an eye on the trail, which was littered with leaves and stones, searching for five-year-old footprints.

As she rounded a bend, she could finally see the yellow tent in the meadow below. It bloomed like a single dandelion in a field of green. "Max!" she called, sprinting down the trail.

When she reached the tent, she tugged at the zipper, trying to get the door open. She pushed herself through the narrow opening, expecting to see Max curled up in a corner. *He'll be sucking his thumb and feeling sorry for himself*, she told herself. *At least I hope so.*

But he wasn't there.

Maggie's heart, still racing from the run here, pounded loudly in her ears. She crawled around the "wall" dividing the two sides of the tent from one another.

Still no Max.

Where was he?

Maggie sat back on her heels, trying to think like her little brother. *If I were Max, where would I hide?* But too many questions popped up. *Why* was he hiding? Why did he run away? What in the world was he crying about in the first place?

She slowly crawled out of the tent and explored the campsite. There were no signs of Max—no fresh muddy footprints, no graham cracker crumbs, no nothing.

Maggie bit her lip. Maybe Max was still back at the lake somewhere. Maybe the others had already found him.

"Please let it be true," she said, crossing her fingers. She dug her heels into the dirt path and started to run.

"You didn't find him?" asked Gran, standing up from the checkered blanket and brushing the crumbs off her lap.

When Maggie saw the worry on Gran's face, she felt a swell of fear in her own chest.

"He's not . . . here?" she asked, trying to catch her breath.

Gran shook her head sadly.

"That's it, then," said Papa, crumpling up his napkin and rising to his feet. "Let's split up and look for him." Papa always knew what to do, and his calm voice reassured Maggie. Together, they would find Max.

Papa, Maggie, and Gabby decided to search the woods near the lake. Gran, Ellie, Ava, and Bella would walk back toward the campsite, exploring the woods along the trail. Maggie had already done that, but maybe she had missed something. Maybe Max was hiding behind a bush or even in the low limbs of a pine tree, and she'd been running by so fast she hadn't seen him.

He's out there somewhere, Maggie thought as she watched Gran disappear over the rise in the trail. *Please let us find him soon.*

"Max!" called Papa, pushing through the brush at the edge of the woods.

Maggie turned and hurried to catch up with him and Gabby. "Max!" she echoed, searching beneath and behind bushes.

Gabby was looking up in the trees as if Max had done a monkey act and climbed up high.

Who knows? thought Maggie. She started looking up, too. But when she wasn't watching the path in front of her, she got hung up on burrs and thorns. "Ouch!" she cried, carefully bending back a prickly branch so she could step past it.

"I know!" called Gabby, who was picking burrs off the front of her T-shirt. "It's like an obstacle course in here."

Papa, though, barreled through the brush like a bear on a berry-finding mission. Maggie tried to follow him. But when the woods gave way to a clearing, the search party had to stop. They'd found no berries—and no little boy.

Papa took a deep breath, stroked the sweat off his moustache, and looked both ways. He was beet red. Tomato red. But, right now, the whole Papa Tomato thing didn't seem so funny to Maggie.

"I think we should turn back, girls," he said, taking off his glasses to clean them with his shirt. "Maybe Gran had better luck finding Max at the campsite."

Maggie turned to look at Gabby, whose worried expression matched her own. The doubt in Papa's voice scared Maggie. Was he starting to lose hope? Was Max really lost?

The girls trudged behind Papa back through the woods, hoping to spot some sign of Max: his red fireman T-shirt or his muddy little cargo pants. But there was nothing.

Papa gathered his fishing pole and tackle box from the lake, and then led the girls down the trail toward the campsite.

How many times today have I taken this trail? wondered Maggie. But instead of counting, she raised her voice like Papa's. "Max!" she called, with every other step.

The name just bounced back to them, sounding hollow, lost, and lonely.

"It's funny," said Maggie, sitting next to Gabby in the grass beside the tent. "A few hours ago, all I could think about was my missing Marsha Mellow. But now?" She fought down the sadness swelling in her throat. "Now, all I can think about is Max. I miss him way more than I miss Marsha Mellow."

Gabby nodded and rested her head on Maggie's shoulder. "I know," she said. "I would be so scared if anything ever happened to Ellie." She lifted her head for a moment to check on her little sister, who was helping Gran collect leaves of different shapes and sizes.

Ava and Bella were standing at the foot of the trail, watching for Papa. He had gone back toward the lake looking for Max—again. Everyone was hoping that any minute now, Papa would come trotting down the trail with Max on his shoulders. But as the sun sank lower in the sky, Maggie was just getting more scared. Really scared.

"What if he's not back by nighttime?" she whispered to Gabby, almost not wanting to say the words out loud.

"But we're supposed to leave before then."

"I know! That's what scares me. We can't leave him here. But how are we going to find him in the dark?"

Gabby shivered. "I don't know. Isn't Max afraid of the dark?"

Maggie nodded. Now she couldn't speak at all. The thought of her little brother alone and scared in the pitch-black was just too much. She looked again toward the trail, hoping that if she just wished hard enough, she could make Papa and her brother appear out of thin air.

"Max is sure good at hiding," Gabby said, trying to lighten the mood. "Remind me never to play hide-and-seek with your brother."

"He is," said Maggie softly. "If only I could figure out why he's hiding—and how to make him come back out."

"Maybe we could whistle for him," said Gabby thoughtfully. She selected a wide blade of grass, plucked it from the ground, and held it between her two thumbs. Then she raised it to her lips and blew against it, creating a loud shrieking whistle.

"Stop!" called Ellie. "I hate that noise!"

Gabby sighed and let the grass fall from her fingers. "Ellie's right," she said. "That sound would probably just scare Max away." She pulled up her knees and rested her chin on top. "What kinds of things does Max like?"

"What do you mean?" asked Maggie.

Gabby shrugged. "Maybe we can do something fun. Something so fun that Max will have to come out of hiding."

Maggie perked up. "Yes! That's a great idea. We could sing a song, maybe—like that John Jacob one."

Gabby's head bobbed up and down. The girls stared at each other for a moment, as though wondering who would sing the first note. Then Maggie opened her mouth and started, quietly at first:

John Jacob Jingleheimer Schmidt,
His name is my *name, too.*

By the time the girls had reached the next few lines, they were singing more clearly and confidently. Ellie ran over and joined in, waving handfuls of leaves in the air like pom-poms.

Whenever we go out,
The people always shout,
"There goes John Jacob Jingleheimer Schmidt!"
Na na na na na na na . . .

They paused before starting the verse again. Maggie searched the bushes around the campsite with her eyes, wishing she would hear one more voice belting out the campfire song. But all was quiet, except for a bird twittering in the treetops overhead.

Gran eyed the girls curiously, and then she seemed to catch on. She began to sing, and even Ava and Bella stepped away from the trail to join in. Everyone raised their voices loudly—loudly enough to carry through the trees all the way to the lake, or to wherever Max was hiding.

"Na na na na na na na . . ." they finished together. And then listened.

They sang the verse again. And listened again.

But eventually, their voices dissolved into silence. No one seemed to have the heart for another round.

Maggie picked at the end of her shoelace. If that song didn't bring Max out of hiding, what would? What would he love even more than singing?

The answer came to her in a single word: Shopkins.

That's what he was always begging to be a part of. So, before the others got totally discouraged, Maggie stood up and announced her new plan.

"Let's play Shopkins," she said firmly.

Gabby looked up at her from the ground as if she'd just lost her mind.

"Right now?" she asked.

"Yes," said Maggie loudly. "Except, you know what? I don't think we have enough people to play. I wish we had one more."

Gabby's eyes lit up. "Right," she said. "I'll bet if Max were here, he'd play with us, wouldn't he?"

"I bet Max would play Shopkins," said Maggie, almost shouting by now. "Too bad he's not here, though. Oh, well."

And that's when she heard it.

A small voice rose above the rustling of the leaves in the breeze.

"I'm here," it said. "I'm over here."

Chapter Nine

Maggie whirled around, trying to track the voice. It was coming from the fire pit—no, past the fire pit. It was coming from the woodpile.

Maggie ran to the stacked logs, with Gabby and the others on her heels. And there, just behind the logs, sat Max, curled up like a lost puppy. His face was still red from crying, and there was a tiny twig dangling from a tuft of his ginger hair.

"Max!"

Maggie pulled him to his feet and gave him the biggest hug she could.

"Stop!" he cried, trying to squirm out of her arms. But she just hugged him tighter.

Then, when he had finally broken free, Maggie felt a different emotion altogether: anger.

"Max!" she scolded him. "Why were you hiding? You scared us!"

When his face scrunched up again, she lowered her voice and knelt in front of him. "It's okay," she said. "Don't cry. Just tell me why you ran away."

But Max wouldn't talk. He crossed his arms and stuck out his lip.

"He'll tell us when he's ready, won't you, Maxxy?" Gran said, reaching for his hand. "For now, why don't you help your old Gran find some pretty leaves? Then we'll have a present for Papa when he gets back."

Max nodded and took Gran's hand.

As Maggie watched them walk away, she crossed her own arms and shook her head. *How can I go from missing Max to being mad at him in about three seconds?* she wondered. But being mad felt better. At least now she knew Max was okay.

"Girls, why don't you start getting your things together?" called Gran over her shoulder. "We'll take the tent down as soon as Papa gets back."

"Aw, man," said Ellie. She wasn't ready for the weekend to be over.

But, Maggie was ready—more than ready—to go home. She suddenly felt really tired. Was it because she'd lost Marsha Mellow? Or because she'd tossed and turned all night with bad dreams? Or because she'd gotten into a fight with two of her closest friends? Or because she'd almost lost her little brother in the woods?

Maybe because of all of it, she thought wearily as she unzipped the tent and crawled inside.

By the time Gran and Max had returned from their leaf gathering, Maggie and her friends had tidied up their half of the tent. The sleeping bags were rolled up, the backpacks were packed, and the duffel bags were zipped shut.

Maggie carried her duffel out of the tent, but Gran raised a hand to stop her just as she emerged from the doorway.

"Max has something he wants to say to you first," said Gran. Her eyes shot Maggie a look that said, *This is hard for him, so try to be nice.*

Max was standing beside Gran, his head hanging low. Now, instead of looking like a lost puppy, he looked like a naughty one who'd just gotten busted for chewing up a slipper.

"O-kay," said Maggie slowly. "What is it, Max?"

He mumbled something, and Gran leaned over. "A little louder, Maxxy," she said, giving his shoulders an encouraging squeeze.

"I took Marsha Mellow," Max repeated. It came out in a whisper, but Maggie heard every word.

"You did *what*?" She nearly dropped her duffel bag. Her friends stepped out of the tent behind her to hear the confession, too.

Gran gave Maggie a pleading look and raised a finger to her lips. "I know it's hard, Margaret," she said, "but just try to hear him out."

Maggie clamped her mouth shut and bit her upper lip to keep from shouting at her little brother.

"Tell her the rest, Max," Grandma nudged.

He started to cry. "I . . . l-lost . . . her," he said, in between great gulps. "I . . . put her in my p-p-pocket . . . and . . . then . . . she was g-gone!"

Maggie's insides felt like they'd been set on fire. Now she couldn't speak at all—she was afraid of what she might say.

"Very good, Max," Grandma said soothingly. "Now, is there just one more thing you need to say to Maggie? One very important thing?"

Max hiccupped and nodded. He wiped his runny nose with the back of his hand. "S-s-sorry," he stammered.

Maggie's cheeks burned. She knew they were as red as Papa Tomato's. All she could do was glare at Max, her eyes like lasers on that wet, snotty face.

Gran lowered her chin to catch Maggie's eyes. "Take some time to think about that apology, Maggie," she said. "We'll talk more when you're ready, okay?"

Then Gran led Max away quickly, as if she were afraid to leave him within Maggie's reach. Gabby and Ellie also tiptoed around Maggie as if they, too, were scared of what she might do.

But when Ava passed by, she looked Maggie directly in the eye. "I guess you found your thief," she snapped. She pushed past Maggie and walked away.

Maggie took a deep, shaky breath. Something about seeing Ava so furious made Maggie feel a little less angry herself.

If Gran had still been standing there, Maggie knew exactly what her grandmother would have said: "I think someone else has an apology to make. . . ."

"I do," Maggie grumbled to herself. "And I will. When I'm ready."

"But why didn't you just ask me if you could play with Marsha Mellow?" asked Maggie, throwing up her hands.

Max picked at a scab on his elbow. They were sitting on a bench in the parking lot while the others waited in the van. Gran had wanted them to talk before starting the long drive home.

What's the point? thought Maggie. *Max is just going to argue with everything I say. And afterward, Marsha Mellow will still be gone.*

"I did ask," Max protested. "I asked if I could play, and you said no. I asked if I could watch, and you said no. I asked if I could listen, and you said—"

"Okay, okay." Maggie raised her hand like a stop sign. "I remember." Sometimes, she wished her little brother didn't have such a perfect memory. "But you still shouldn't have stolen her," she said, feeling her blood start to boil again.

"I didn't steal her," said Max. "I just wanted to play with her. I put her in my pocket. And then, later, when I went to bring her back to you, she was . . ." He began to sniffle.

"I know that part," Maggie said. "She was missing."

Max nodded miserably.

"Well, why did you want to play with her, anyway?" Maggie asked. "Don't you know Shopkins are for girls?"

Max winced as if she'd just slapped him. No boys Max's age wanted to be caught playing with girl toys.

Maggie knew those words would sting. She almost felt bad about saying them. Almost.

Instead of apologizing, though, she glanced toward the van full of people waiting in the parking lot. She could just about make out the faces of her friends through those tinted windows. She was sure they were all watching and waiting.

But what more was there to say?

Maggie pushed off from the bench and walked toward the van. She could feel Max trotting behind at her heels. He was probably thrilled that the conversation was over.

As the van pulled out of the parking lot, Maggie pressed her forehead against the cool windowpane. She watched the trees of Crystal Lake Woods slide by and slowly disappear from view.

At least now, Maggie thought, *I finally know who took Marsha Mellow.*

The only problem was, she still had no idea where the Shopkin was.

And she was pretty certain that she'd never see Marsha Mellow again.

Chapter Ten

Teasley Toys, the most magical place on earth, had somehow lost its magic.

Maggie searched every inch of the store, trying to figure out what had changed. The bookshelf just inside the front door was still painted with every color of the rainbow, but the colors looked faded and worn. The stuffed animals flopped lifelessly on the shelves, staring at Maggie through their dull glass eyes.

Even the red train had lost its luster. When Maggie turned it on, it circled the tracks once and then . . . *whir, whir, whir*. It got hung up on the crooked track and refused to budge.

Maggie's shoulders slumped as she flipped the switch to off. She trudged to the back room and flopped down in Gran's desk chair.

"What's the matter, Magpie?" asked Papa, who was helping Gran unpack a new shipment. "You look like a droopy rag doll."

Maggie shrugged.

"This will perk her up," said Gran. She slid her scissors along the top of a brown cardboard box. As the box popped open, she folded back the top flaps and let Maggie get a glimpse of the pink packages inside.

Ah, Shopkins. Maggie would recognize those packages anywhere, but today, even those couldn't lift her spirits.

Gran looked puzzled. "Want to help me arrange them in the display?" she asked, trying again.

Maggie nodded slowly. She didn't want to hurt Gran's feelings, and if she was going to be moping around the toy store, she might as well help out.

It was Monday night—only one day since the camping weekend. But Maggie felt like a gloomy cloud had followed her from the campsite all the way home.

As she put the Shopkins five-packs in tidy rows in the bin, Maggie barely looked at the characters inside: Wendy Washer, Betty Boot, Chris P Crackers. What did it matter? She probably wouldn't ever get Marsha Mellow again.

Even if she did, she'd still be mad at Max for messing with her things.

And Ava will still be mad at me, thought Maggie sadly.

"What did he want with her anyway?" she suddenly asked out loud.

"Hmm?" said Gran, tidying up the tray of tiny Shopkins baskets on the checkout counter.

"Why did Max want to play with Marsha Mellow? I mean, it's a girl's toy," Maggie complained.

"Oh, I don't know," said Gran. "He knows how much you care about your Shopkins. Maybe he just wanted to see what all the fuss was about."

Maggie ran her finger around the scalloped shell of the package she was holding. "That's dumb," she said. "I know how much he cares about his remote-control cars, but that doesn't mean that I want to play with them. I couldn't care less about those!"

There was no response. Gran was lost in thought, checking off what she called "inventory" on her clipboard. Her lips were moving as if she were doing business in her head.

So when Papa came out of the back room carrying a tower of stacked cardboard boxes,

Maggie asked him, too. "Why do you think Max wanted to play with my Marsha Mellow? It's totally a girl's toy."

Papa carefully placed the boxes beside the Shopkins bin. "What's that?" he asked, pulling a hankie out of his pants pocket to wipe his face.

Maggie sighed and repeated her question. It was hard to get anyone to listen to her today, and this was important!

Papa lifted one of the Shopkins packages out of the bin and studied it. "What makes this a girl's toy?" he asked thoughtfully. "Is it just because the package is pink?"

"Well, yeah!" said Maggie, as if he'd just asked if the sky were blue. "Plus, boys don't really collect little things like Shopkins."

Papa stroked his moustache. "Now, I know that's not true, Magpie," he said. "I collected things like this when I was a boy."

Papa playing with Shopkins? Maggie smothered a giggle. "You did not," she said.

Papa nodded. "I sure did!" he said, his eyes twinkling behind his round glasses. "I'll prove it to you. Follow me."

He walked toward the back room, and Maggie followed close on his heels. She still thought he was joking around with her, trying to make her feel better. But now she was curious.

Along with Gran's big desk and that rainbow rug, the back room had two tall white cabinets. Maggie knew that one of the cabinets stored cleaning supplies. She'd often helped Gran clean the top of the checkout counter or wipe the glass of the front door and windows.

But Maggie had never seen what was in the second cabinet. When Papa pulled some keys out of his pocket, she held her breath and watched him unlock the cabinet.

The door swung open with a groan, and Papa studied the shelves. Instead of cleaning or office supplies, these shelves held toys. Maggie could tell from where she stood that they weren't new toys in fresh packages. They were well-worn and loved.

A cloth doll with stitched eyes sat propped up on one shelf, her striped legs dangling over the edge. Beside her, a pink metal oven held tiny pots and pans on its burners. Below that, a jar of glass marbles caught the light, casting a soft, colorful glow onto the inside wall of the cabinet.

"These," Papa announced, "are some of the toys your Gran and I used to love when we were little. They remind us of what kids still love today. How about that, Magpie? Your old Gran and Papa were kids once upon a time. Can you imagine?"

Maggie shook her head. She couldn't picture Papa as a little boy. She couldn't imagine him without his moustache, or with hair on the top of his head. She wondered if he'd looked like Max when he was little.

But she didn't spend long thinking about it. She was too curious about these old toys.

Papa reached for something on the top shelf. He carefully slid out what looked like a green metal tackle box. "Ah, there you are," he said affectionately, as if talking to an old friend.

Papa set the box down on Gran's desk. "C'mon," he said to Maggie, waving her over beside him. "This hasn't been opened in years, so this is a big moment."

Maggie was beside him in an instant, peering down at the metal box. She felt like a deep sea diver, about to open a sunken treasure chest.

Papa wiped a layer of dust off the top of the box. Then he popped the latch with his thumb and swung open the lid.

Maggie recognized the contents as soon as she saw them: piles of little plastic soldiers. Some were green and some were gray, but otherwise, they all looked the same. She'd seen something similar lined up on the shelf of a thrift shop a few years ago.

Her stomach sunk with disappointment. How were these anything like Shopkins?

But as Papa lifted the soldiers out of the box, one by one, Maggie realized they weren't all the same. Each man was standing a little bit differently. Some held weapons, and others did not.

Papa arranged them on the desk like soldiers on a battlefield: some facing each other and others fighting side by side. "These," he said proudly, "were mine when I was Max's age. These were *my* Shopkins."

Maggie snorted—she couldn't help it. These plastic soldiers sure didn't look like Shopkins! They weren't nearly as fun or as colorful.

But as Papa placed more soldiers tenderly on the desk, she could see that he cared a lot about them. For just a moment, in her mind, she saw Papa as a little boy. He had freckles, like Max, and he stuck his tongue out when he was concentrating, like Max did sometimes. Maggie smiled.

Then the little boy turned toward her, and he was Papa again.

"Do you still think boys don't 'collect little things'?" he asked, grinning at her.

She shook her head. But something was still bothering her.

"Some little boys might like things like this," she said, pointing toward the tiny green and gray army. "But Max doesn't."

"How do you know?" asked Papa, straightening up in the desk chair. "Maybe he's been trying to tell you that he does."

Maggie stared deep into Papa's wise eyes, seeing a hint of her reflection in his glasses. He was probably right. Papa was usually right.

But did that mean Maggie had to share her Shopkins with Max?

Her eyes flickered away from Papa's and back to the battlefield laid out on the desk before her. Maggie focused on one single soldier, who stood off to the side alone.

Just like me, thought Maggie.

Sometimes it seemed like everyone was against her, and she was fighting a battle on her own. Against Max. Against Ava. And now, even against Papa.

She wanted to do the right thing—she really did—but why did it feel so hard?

Chapter Eleven

When Friday afternoon rolled around, those toy soldiers were all packed up and back in the cabinet. Papa probably didn't want to lose them.

I know how he feels, thought Maggie sadly, tightening the grip on the new Shopkins basket she held in her hand. She had already lost one special Shopkin. She was determined not to lose another.

So far, Gabby and Ellie were the only other members of the Shopkins Kids Club who had arrived. They were digging around in the Shopkins bin, trying to pick out their purchases.

"Don't mess those up!" Maggie almost said. She and Gran had worked so hard to line them up perfectly on Monday. But she didn't scold her friends. She was too busy watching the front door. Where were Ava and Bella?

Will they even come? Maggie wondered. She hadn't talked to Ava all week, even though she'd seen her riding her bike and had waved to her. Ava had just stared straight ahead. How long could a girl stay mad, anyway?

She saw Bella's face through the glass just as she heard the *jingle* of the front door opening. Maggie was shocked to see Bella push through the door first. Where was Ava? Maggie craned her neck to see behind Bella's springy curls.

"Oh, hi," said Bella shyly, as if she were surprised to see Maggie waiting for her.

"Hi, Bella!" said Ellie, waving with a Shopkins package in her hand.

"Where's Ava?" asked Gabby.

Bella's dark eyes dropped to her feet. "She's not coming," she said quietly. "I, um, can't stay either. I just wanted to come to tell you."

She looked up at Maggie, gave an apologetic little shrug, and then darted out the door almost as quickly as she'd appeared. Her mom must have been waiting in the car at the curb.

"Who's here?" asked Gran, hurrying in from the back room. "Did I miss a customer?"

"Nope," said Maggie sadly. "It was just Bella."

"Oh," said Gran, glancing around the room in confusion. "Where is she? Is she coming back?"

Maggie shook her head. "I don't think so. I think it's just the four of us today." *And every Friday from here till eternity*, she thought as she led her friends into the back room.

The Shopkins Kids Club had never felt quite so small. As the girls sat down in a tight little circle, Maggie said, "Well, who wants to go first?"

Gabby scrunched up her forehead. "What do you mean?" she asked. "You're supposed to check your notebook and tell us!"

"Oh, right," said Maggie. She got to her feet and slid the lime green notebook and a pen out of the desk drawer. She flipped it open and studied the last page. "Um, Ellie went first last time, so you go first today, Gabby."

Maggie was relieved it wasn't Ava's or Bella's turn to go first. It just wouldn't feel right skipping over them.

Gabby used scissors to snip open her first yellow pouch. When a Shopkin dropped out, she picked him up and lifted him closer to her face. "Aw, what a cute little green dude," she said, smiling.

"That's Dippy Avocado," said Maggie, unfolding the checklist taped to her green notebook. "He is . . . common," she said, reading the checklist.

Gabby nodded. When she opened the other yellow pouch, she recognized the Shopkin right away, and so did Maggie—Slick Breadstick.

Gabby and Maggie locked eyes. Were they both remembering last Friday, when Ava and Bella had opened Slick Breadstick? When they'd added him to the Slick Breadstick they'd already had in their collection and called them "twinsies"? The memory stung a little. Maggie had to look away from Gabby's gaze.

Ellie bounced on her heels. "Okay, your turn, Maggie!" she said. She was the only one here who was acting normal. Ellie could find a way to be cheery even if the sky were falling. Maggie was grateful for that.

"Okay, Ellie, hold your horses," she said, reaching for her own plastic basket. "Where are the scissors?"

"Just rip it open!" said Ellie.

"Jeepers, Ellie," said Gabby, putting her hand on her sister's head. "Settle down, already!"

Maggie wished she shared Ellie's excitement. But today, as she snipped the corner of her first yellow pouch, the only thing she could muster up was a little curiosity. The Shopkin stuck in the corner of the pouch, so she reached in to fish it out.

"Corny Cob!" cheered Ellie, as she peeked over Maggie's shoulder.

Sure enough, it was a cute little ear of corn.

"He's rare," said Ellie.

"How do you know that?" asked Gabby.

Ellie just shrugged. But she was right. Maggie looked at the checklist, and Corny Cob had a green circle next to him.

"Yup, she's rare all right," said Maggie, using her pen to check the Shopkin off her list. She liked to keep track of which ones she had and which ones she was still waiting for.

"*He* is rare," Ellie corrected her, raising a finger. "Corny Cob is a boy."

Maggie held up the Shopkin so she could study his face. He didn't have long eyelashes. He did look kind of like a boy.

As she opened her next yellow pouch, a strange-looking Shopkin fell out. All three girls leaned forward, staring at the purple and blue rectangle resting on the rainbow rug.

"Is that a saw?" asked Gabby, tilting her head for a better view.

"I don't know," said Maggie, picking him up. She scanned her checklist. "Oh!" she said. "It's Al Foil." The "saw" was actually a sheet of aluminum foil being pulled from a little cardboard tube.

"He's a boy, too," said Ellie with certainty.

"Who cares?" said Gabby impatiently. "Is he common or rare?"

"Or ultra rare?" added Ellie. "He could be ultra rare, Gabby." She gave her sister a knowing look.

Gabby rolled her eyes and let out an exasperated sigh.

Maggie checked her list again. "He's . . . common," she said. But she wasn't really disappointed. She was suddenly curious to know just how many boy Shopkins she had in her collection.

She barely watched Ellie take her turn, which seemed okay by Ellie. She had both pouches open in no time. "Oh, man!" she said. "I already have these!" She held up Squeaky Clean and Bart Beans.

"No, Ellie," said Gabby, pointing toward the spray bottle. "You have the blue Squeaky Clean. This one's yellow."

"Oh," said Ellie, her eyes lighting up. "Oh, yeah! But Bart Beans is a trader. Who wants to trade?"

"Just a sec. Let me see what I have," said Gabby, pulling open her plastic bag of Shopkins.

But Maggie beat her to the punch. "I'll take him," she said quickly, searching through her bag for duplicates.

Maggie had a plan, and for the first time in two days, she was suddenly feeling a whole lot better.

Whoo, whoo! That was Maggie's cue that Mom and Max had finally arrived at the toy shop. Max usually went straight to the train set first.

Finally! Maggie thought, checking the clock on the wall. Gabby and Ellie had been picked up ten minutes ago, which felt like ten hours ago.

"Max!" she called to her brother from the back room. "Come in here for a minute!"

"Just a sec," he said, kneeling by the train tracks.

"Max!" said Maggie impatiently. She marched into the store and took Max by the hand.

"What's the big rush?" asked Mom, eyeing Maggie suspiciously.

"Nothing," said Maggie. "I just have a surprise that I know Max will like."

That made her little brother's feet move more quickly toward the back room. He loved surprises!

Maggie told him to sit down at Gran's desk. Then she made her big announcement.

"Maxwell," she said, standing before him, "I've decided that it's time for you to have your very own Shopkins."

Her little brother's smile faded. "No," he said, lowering his head. "That's okay. I know Shopkins are for girls."

Maggie sighed. "Actually, Max," she said, kneeling in front of him, "I was wrong about that. I'm sorry."

Max didn't look convinced. He stared at her with cautious green eyes, like she was trying to trick him or something.

Maggie couldn't really blame him for that, after all the fighting they'd done lately. "Here," she said, "I'll prove it to you." She reached into the desk drawer where she kept the lime green Shopkins notebook. Then she pulled out a small plastic bag of Shopkins.

"Meet . . . Bart Beans," said Maggie, placing a small yellow can on the desk. "And here's one of his friends, Corny Cob. He tells corny jokes, just like you."

Max giggled at that and reached for the tiny corn of cob. "He's a boy?" he asked, holding the Shopkin carefully between his fingers.

Maggie smiled. "Yup, and so is this guy." She added Al Foil to the row of Shopkins, lined up on the desktop like Papa's soldiers.

Max cocked his head. "Is that a saw?" he asked.

Maggie laughed. "No, but he looks like one, doesn't he?"

Max nodded. "He's cute. I like him. I like all of them." He rested his chin on the desk to get a better look at the Shopkins.

"I thought you might," said Maggie. "And that's why I'm giving them to you."

A moment passed, and then Max's head popped back up. "All of them?" he asked, his eyes wide.

"All of them," said Maggie. "You can start your own collection!"

When Max's face broke into a huge smile, Maggie's heart swelled in her chest. "I'm glad you like them, Maxxy," she said. "But make sure not to lose them!"

He shook his head. "I won't!" He picked up the Shopkins and started to tuck them into the top pocket of his cargo pants. That's when Maggie saw the white smudge on his knees.

"What is that?" she said, rubbing her finger along the smudge. It was sticky.

"Marshmallow," said Max, matter-of-factly.

"Gross!" said Maggie, wiping her hand on her shorts. "Are those the same pants you wore to the campout? Didn't you let Mom wash them for you?"

Max raised his shoulders and cocked his head to the side.

Boys sure like dirt, thought Maggie. *But they like Shopkins, too*, she reminded herself. So she helped Max "collect" his new collection from the desk.

"Here, put them in this pocket," she said, pointing to the wide lower pocket by Max's knee. "This one has a button, so you can close it and keep the Shopkins safe."

Max nodded and lifted his leg so Maggie could unbutton the flap. But the pocket felt lumpy. It already had something inside.

She reached her hand in and groped around from side to side. When her fingers touched the square plastic figure, she caught her breath.

Maggie knew exactly what was in that pocket waiting for her.

Marsha Mellow.

Chapter Twelve

"Marsha Mellow!"

Max seemed just as surprised as Maggie was to see the toasty little marshmallow—and, just as happy. He hopped off the chair, and he and Maggie did a little dance in the storage room.

"What on earth is going on in here?" asked Gran, poking her gray head through the doorway.

Maggie held up her Shopkin. "Look who's back, Gran!" she sang.

Gran slid her lavender glasses up onto her nose and inspected the Shopkin. "Well, if I didn't know better, I'd say that was our friend . . ."

"Marsha Mellow!" all three said together.

"Well, it's about time!" said Gran, wagging her finger and pretending to scold the little Shopkin. "We were worried about you, Miss Marsha."

"Look, Gran!" said Max, running back toward the desk. He gathered up his three new Shopkins to show her. "Maggie gave me my own Shopkins."

"Did she now?" said Gran, casting a sideways glance at Maggie.

When Max ran out of the room to show Mom his new Shopkins, Gran put her arm around Maggie and pulled her close. "I'm very proud of you, Margaret," she said. "And I know that Papa will be, too."

Maggie nodded and pressed her cheek against Gran's warm shoulder. Then she held up Marsha Mellow, turning the Shopkin from side to side so the bling caught the light of the lamp overhead.

There's still one more thing I have to do, though, she thought. *Then, maybe I can feel proud of myself, too.*

As Maggie climbed up the porch steps of the big gray house, she heard the hum of her mom's car engine from the street below. The sound comforted her and gave her the courage to reach up and ring the doorbell.

A woman answered the door, a woman with wide-set eyes and curly hair. It was Ava and Bella's mother. "Oh, hi, Maggie," she said. "Here, let me call the girls."

"Wait!" said Maggie. "I just need to talk to Ava for a moment—I mean, if she'll let me."

Ava's mother gave Maggie a curious look, as if she had no idea what she was talking about. That meant Ava hadn't told her mother about the fight. She hadn't tattled on Maggie, just like she hadn't tattled to Gran the morning she'd busted Maggie going through her things in the tent.

Ava is actually a pretty loyal friend, thought Maggie. That made her feel sad—and guilty—for ever thinking Ava would steal from her. *But today, I'm going to make it right*, Maggie reminded herself. She stood a little taller as she waited by the door.

Ava's eyes looked wary when she came outside and saw Maggie standing there. She zipped up her hoodie and stepped onto the porch, closing the door behind her.

"What do you want, Maggie?" she asked, folding her arms across her chest.

Maggie took a deep breath. "I'm here to say I'm sorry. I'm really, really sorry that I thought you took my Marsha Mellow." She looked Ava straight in the eyes, hoping her friend could see just how guilty she felt.

Ava looked away first, as if she didn't know what to do with the apology. She glanced over Maggie's shoulder at the car waiting in the street below.

"It's fine, Maggie," she said, shifting uncomfortably. "I know your mom probably made you say that."

"No!" said Maggie quickly. "She didn't. It was my idea to come here. I wanted to give you something."

"What?" asked Ava. She sounded like Max did when Maggie first tried to give him some Shopkins. Ava didn't trust Maggie—at least, not yet.

Maggie held out her closed hand. *Here goes nothing*, she thought to herself. *Please take it, Ava. Please!*

Ava hesitated, but she finally held out her own hand, palm up.

Maggie didn't waste a second before dropping something into Ava's palm.

"Marsha Mellow," whispered Ava, staring down at the Shopkin. "You found her!"

"I did," said Maggie. "My little brother had her all along."

Ava jerked her head up. "Really? He stole her and kept her?"

"No," said Maggie, shaking her head. "Nobody stole her. He just lost her—in a pair of pants that had way too many pockets."

Ava flashed a grin and glanced down at Marsha Mellow. She grew more serious, then, and said, "I can't take her."

Maggie blinked once, then twice. *If Ava won't take Marsha Mellow, how can I make things right?*

"I can't take her," Ava repeated, "but I can trade you for her—a fair trade this time. Wait here, okay?"

Ava ducked back into her doorway, and Maggie could hear the sound of her footsteps on the stairs. A few minutes later, she came back with her Shopkins lunchbox.

"Let's sit down," said Ava, gesturing toward the porch steps.

Maggie gladly sat beside her. She could see Mom in the car down below, leaning forward as if to make sure everything was all right.

Maggie raised her finger to say "Just a minute!" This was important Shopkins Kids Club business. She knew Mom would understand.

As Ava popped open the lunchbox on her lap, Maggie noticed that it looked kind of like Papa's metal box of soldiers. The Shopkins in this box were much more colorful than those green and gray soldiers, but Maggie knew that Papa loved his collection just as much as Ava loved hers.

Will Ava and I keep our collections as long as Papa kept his? she wondered. She hoped so. She thought so. How could she ever part with her Shopkins?

From the corner of the lunchbox, Ava pulled out a small plastic bag of special Shopkins. Maggie could see right away that these were the limited-edition ones with the bling. There were five or six Shopkins in the bag.

Now Maggie knew exactly why Ava wanted Marsha Mellow. She had just about every other limited-edition Shopkin. With Marsha Mellow, she'd have the whole set!

"Which one do you want?" asked Ava.

Maggie shook her head. "If you trade one," she said, "you won't have them all."

Ava hesitated and chewed her lip. It looked like she was still making a decision—a very important decision—in her mind. "That's okay," she finally said. "Bella and I will get more someday."

Maggie stared at her friend. *Who is this girl?*

She glanced back down at the bag. She could see that Ava had a set of "twinsies"—two of the tiniest limited-edition Shopkins. "Are those lemons?" Maggie asked, pointing.

"Those are both Lenny Lime," said Ava, fishing one of the little guys out of the bag. "But you don't have to take him just because I have two."

Maggie reached out to hold the sparkly little lime. "That's okay," she said. "This is actually the one I want."

Ava leaned backward, examining Maggie's face as if to see if she were telling the truth. She must have been convinced, because she smiled. She looked a little relieved, too, that Maggie hadn't chosen one of the others.

"Okay, then. It's a fair trade!" Ava announced. She handed Lenny Lime to Maggie. Then she gazed lovingly at Marsha Mellow, kissed her toasty little head, and dropped her carefully into the bag.

By the time Ava had closed her Shopkins lunchbox and locked it tight, she was looking like her old self again.

Finally, thought Maggie. All was right with the world.

She leaned in and gave Ava a quick hug. "I'd better go," she said, nodding toward her mom's car. She started down the steps, but stopped and turned. "Ava?" she called back over her shoulder.

"Yeah?" Ava was standing by her front door.

"Will I see you next Friday?" Maggie asked, hoping more than anything that Ava's answer would be yes.

Ava's face broke into a smile. She nodded happily. "Yup," she said. And then she added, "Check you later!"

"Check you later!" called Maggie. As she bounded down the steps, she felt the sun on her face. That gloomy cloud from last weekend had moved on at last.

As she reached for the handle of her mom's car door, she squeezed Lenny Lime tightly in her hand. She didn't want to lose the Shopkin now. She was about to give her—no *him*—to a brand-new collector, a boy who would love him just as much as she did.